LADYBUG LABYRINTH FOR 1

Ladybug Labyrinth:
a journey home

Lea Goode-Harris, Ph.D.

Published by G & H Publishing
© 2006 Santa Rosa Labyrinth Foundation
www.srlabyrinthfoundation.com

Ladybug Labyrinth:
a journey home

Design and illustrations by Lea Goode-Harris, Ph.D.

Cover and inside front cover:
Three-circuit Classical Grass Labyrinth by Lea Goode-Harris

Inside back cover:
Double-Entrance Meander Classical Grass Labyrinth by Lea Goode-Harris

Special thanks to Chaela Sumner and John McKenzie
of Sumner McKenzie, Inc.

Second edition
©2006, Lea Goode-Harris, Ph.D.
ISBN: 0-9762054-4-0

Published by G & H Publishing
Santa Rosa Labyrinth Foundation

website: www.srlabyrinthfoundation.com
e-mail: goodeharris@gmail.com

*To Ladybugs… and all beings
precious and small…*

Who
Flies on tiny
Wings beneath
A cloak of red?

Little dot of nature
Lights upon my fingertip
And whispers
Stories
To me
Of ladybugs
And the journey
Home...

Ladybug Labyrinth:
a journey home

CONTENTS

Dedication... 3

Poem: Who Flies?.. 4

Ladybug Labyrinth: a journey home... 7

Ladybug Labyrinth: for 1 and for 2.. 20

Ladybugs, Labyrinths, and Resources..................................... 21

About the Author.. 24

Ladybug Labyrinth:
a journey home

Once,

there was a little,

   teensie-weenie

   ladybug.

      One morning,

        Ladybug decided to go

          on an adventure,

           for she loved to ride the sky-blue breezes

          of change.

She took off,

    her little wings carrying her

    up into those sky breezes.

This morning though,
the winds blew and blew…
Ladybug was tumbled this way,

 and then that way,

upside down

then right side up,
until Ladybug had no idea
where she was!

Finally,

    Ladybug was able to land

on a splendid blade of grass

    next to a dandelion

and looked around.

She saw birds in the sky,

    she saw a squirrel run up a tree,

    she saw green moss and ferns growing,

and then she saw a sign…

    a wooden sign

    near a bunch of lupine…

The sign said…

So Ladybug got up,
even though she was still
a little bit dizzy,
and followed the sign…

11

She followed the directions

down a path that took

her to another sign.

This one said…

What do you think

Ladybug did?

She went into the labyrinth,

    following the yellow-green path,

edged with waving grass,

    covered in morning dew,

        and moved her little legs gleefully,

as the grasses tickled her legs and belly.

    She wound around

        and around

    and thought she was lost…

but a little voice whispered to her,

    "Don't be afraid,

        trust your feet,"

          so Ladybug continued on…

She turned another corner,

now where was she going?

Was she lost?

The little voice whispered again,

"Trust your feet *and* your fingers,"

and ladybug went on and on…

When ladybug

turned the next corner,

there it was,

the center of the labyrinth

and it was full of golden grass

and daisies.

Ladybug

　　　sat down at the very center

　　　of the labyrinth

　　　and felt the sun beaming down

　　　　　on her shiny back.

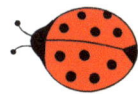

As she wiggled down into the golden center,

Ladybug decided to take a little nap,

　　　for Ladybug was warm and felt safe,

　　　all cozy in the center place.

When Ladybug woke up,

she was rested and happy,

and no longer felt dizzy

or lost,

for she knew right where she was,

in the center place.

What should she do now?

Ladybug wondered.

"Follow the path back home

and take this safe and cozy feeling with you,"

the little voice whispered.

Ladybug asked, "Who are you little voice?"

"I am the voice of your heart," the little voice said.

"And I will always be with you,

especially when you take the time

to slow down and listen..."

So Ladybug

began to wind her way back out of the labyrinth

first turning one way,

then turning another way,

skipping the whole way

for Ladybug knew she couldn't get lost,

following the path

beneath her little legs.

When Ladybug emerged from the labyrinth
she turned around
and blew a kiss to the waving green grass,
"Good-bye labyrinth," Ladybug called,
"I'll come and play again soon."
And with that,
Ladybug unfurled her little wings
and took off again into the sky-blue breezes,
with her heart singing
all the way home.

Ladybug Labyrinths: for 1 or for 2

Ladybug Labyrinth for one and Ladybug Labyrinth for two, on the inside cover pages, can be used as finger labyrinths for children of all ages.

LADYBUG LABYRINTH FOR 1 is a three-circuit classical labyrinth.
 *(see inside front cover.)*

This labyrinth is intended for play, to help focus, to self-soothe, for identifying emotions, feelings, and ideas, or to inspire creativity and curiosity.

LADYBUG LABYRINTH FOR 2 is created from a meander switch back, a pattern found in nature and crafted into a labyrinthine path (see inside back cover). This labyrinth, with double entrances, is for one, two, or more children and is intended to inspire ideas for games and solutions on how they can share the path with each other. A single child can also use this labyrinth.

Both of these labyrinths are available on 12-inch by 12-inch canvas and come with their own ladybug! A hand-painted 12-foot by 15-foot canvas labyrinth for children (and adults) to walk and play on is also available. For more information, visit the Santa Rosa Labyrinth website: www.srlabyrinthfoundation.com

LADYBUGS

Ladybugs don't have actual feet and fingers like you do! Ladybugs are also called "lady birds" or "lady beetles." There are about 5,000 species of ladybugs found around the world! Ladybugs come in different colors, some with spots and some without spots. They're small, usually less than a ¼ of an inch, and oval in shape. Ladybugs are both male and female, with the females a little larger than the males. Ladybugs have six legs, wings to fly, and use their antennae to touch, smell, and to taste.

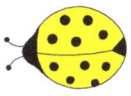

To learn more about ladybugs, a grown-up can help you look them up at your school or public library. Use the internet to do a ladybug search or visit ladybug websites like: http://animals.nationalgeographic.com/animals/bugs/ladybug

LABYRINTHS

Labyrinths are new and old and found through history and around the world. Labyrinths can teach you about yourself, your family and friends, and the world around you. When you walk a labyrinth you can follow the path all the way into the center and back out again. Or you can walk on the lines. You can explore how walking the lines is different from following the path.

Use your imagination when you walk, or finger-walk, a labyrinth. You can make up games, you can sing, you can dance, or you can just be quiet in a labyrinth. You can use a finger-labyrinth, or make a labyrinth on paper, or in y o u r yard. A grown-up can help you use the internet to find a public labyrinth near you at: www.labyrinthlocator.com

Further Labyrinth Resources

The Santa Rosa Labyrinth Foundation
Home of the Santa Rosa Labyrinth, Ladybug Labyrinth, and Resources
www.srlabyrinthfoundation.com

The International Labyrinth Society
www.labyrinthsociety.com

Veriditas
www.veriditas.org

The Worldwide Labyrinth Locator
Jointly created by the Labyrinth Society and Veriditas™ with a grant from the Faith, Hope, and Charity Foundation
www.labyrinthlocator.com

Labyrinthos
The Labyrinth Resource Centre, Photo Library, and Archive
www.labyrinthos.net

Lea Goode-Harris, Ph. D.

Lea Goode-Harris is the Founder of the Santa Rosa Labyrinth Foundation and the artist-creator of the Santa Rosa Labyrinth, widely installed in public and private spaces, and spiritual centers, throughout the world.

In 2002, she designed the Snoopy Labyrinth for the Charles M. Schulz Museum and Research Center in Santa Rosa, California, and in 2005, the Ladybug Labyrinth. Her research on the psychological applications of the labyrinth form the foundation of an innovative method of personal development using the Santa Rosa, as well as traditional, labyrinth designs.

Lea lectures and directs workshops focused on labyrinths, with a goal of facilitating human potential by supporting integration of opposites, and releasing personal creativity through diverse mediums. She also provides consultation on the installation and applications of labyrinths. Her clients have included students and leaders in the fields of education, psychotherapy, and commerce. She has a special interest in working with children and adolescents.

Lea may be contacted through her website at: www.srlabyrinthfoundation.com

LADYBUG LABYRINTH FOR 2